Danger on Ice

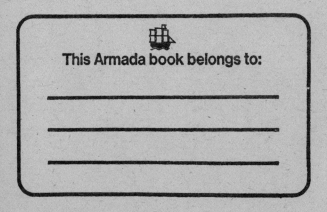

This Armada book belongs to:

_____

_____

_____

There are many fantastic mystery stories in the Nancy Drew series by Carolyn Keene and the Hardy Boys series by Franklin W. Dixon. Have you read them all?

Also available in the *Be A Detective* series:
THE SECRET OF THE KNIGHT'S SWORD

NANCY DREW ® AND THE HARDY BOYS ®
Be A Detective Mystery Stories™

Danger on Ice

Carolyn Keene and
Franklin W. Dixon

Illustrated by Paul Frame

Armada

First published in the U.S.A.
in 1984 by Wanderer Books,
a division of Simon & Schuster, Inc.
First published in the U.K.
in 1985 in Armada by Fontana Paperbacks,
8 Grafton Street, London W1X 3LA.

© Stratemeyer Syndicate 1984

'The Hardy Boys', 'Nancy Drew',
'Nancy Drew Mystery Stories', and 'Be A Detective Mystery Stories'
are trademarks of Stratemeyer Syndicate,
registered in the United States Patent and Trademark Office.

Printed and bound in Great Britain by
Anchor Brendon Ltd, Tiptree, Essex.

Dear Fans,

Since so many of you have written to us saying how much you want to be detectives like Nancy Drew and The Hardy Boys, we figured out a way. Of course, we had to put our heads together to create mysteries that were so baffling they needed help from everyone including Nancy, Frank, Joe and you!

In these exciting new BE A DETECTIVE MYSTERY STORIES you'll be part of a great team of amateur sleuths following clues and wily suspects. At every turn you'll have a chance to pick a different trail filled with adventure that may lead to danger, surprise or an amazing discovery!

The choices are all yours—see how many there are and have fun!

C.K. and F.W.D.

"**H**urray for Kristy!" Nancy Drew exclaimed.

She was watching her hometown friend, Kristy Anderson, step onto the winner's platform in the ice arena in Innsbruck, Austria. An official placed the gold medal for the figure-skating title around the young American's neck. Then the audience erupted into wild applause, led by the loud cheering of Frank and Joe Hardy, who sat next to Nancy.

"She's headed for the Olympics!" Frank said proudly.

"Let's hurry down to meet her," Joe added, "before she's mobbed by fans."

Nancy nodded, and the three young detectives moved through the excited crowd to an exit. They ran down a flight of stairs to the ground floor, where the skaters prepared for their performances.

"Here's her dressing room," Nancy said, pushing open the door. As she entered, she stared into the icy blue eyes of a blond man lurking inside.

"Who are you?" Nancy demanded.

Turn to page 3.

Instead of answering, the stranger rushed out the door, pushing aside Frank and Joe, who were too startled to stop him. Seconds later, he disappeared into the crowd of fans surrounding the champion skater, who at that moment was walking out of the arena.

"Don't mention him to Kristy right now," Nancy whispered to the Hardys. "I don't want to spoil her moment of victory."

"Right," Frank agreed. "But I'll keep my eyes open in case he shows up again."

Just then, the young skater saw her friends and flashed them a victorious smile. Nancy ran up and gave her an affectionate hug, and Frank and Joe warmly congratulated her on her performance.

"Miss Anderson," a photographer called out from the crowd, "a picture, please."

Kristy turned to the camera and proudly held up her gold medal. Soon, she was besieged by reporters' questions.

"What about the Olympics?" one asked. "Do you think you can win the gold there?"

Kristy answered him with calm confidence. Nancy watched her high-school friend admiringly, but in the back of her mind she worried about the man in the dressing room.

Turn to page 4.

Half an hour later, Kristy escaped the reporters and fans and went to change out of her skating costume.

"Let's stay close to her," Frank suggested as they waited. "We don't know what that guy was up to."

Kristy emerged from the dressing room with her skates slung over her shoulders. "I'm ready," she said cheerily.

The four young Americans stepped out into the crisp Austrian evening. They walked to the parking lot where their rented cars were waiting. Nancy slipped behind the wheel of the red Volkswagen with Kristy beside her. Joe climbed into the white Ford sedan his brother was driving.

The two cars started off toward Igles, a small village perched on a mountainside above Innsbruck, where the four were staying. Nancy had accompanied Kristy to her skating competition when their mutual friend, George Fayne, couldn't make the trip. Frank and Joe were in Austria on a ski vacation while their investigator father, Fenton Hardy, worked on an assignment in nearby Geneva.

"This is tricky driving," dark-haired Frank muttered to his brother as the light snow began to fall. "It's hard to get traction on this stuff."

Turn to page 5.

Ahead of them, the brothers watched Nancy maneuver her small car on the slippery surface. Then they saw something that made them catch their breath.

A snowmobile suddenly shot across the road in front of the red VW. Nancy had to swerve sharply to the side to avoid a collision while Frank hit the brakes and pulled up behind her. As the boys got out, they could see the driver of the snowmobile watching the scene intently from a short distance away. The man's face was hidden by his dark bubble helmet, but Joe noted that his snowmobile was yellow with black stripes along its side.

A moment later, the stranger started up his motor and shot off across the snow. Knowing it was impossible to pursue him, Joe and Frank immediately checked on Nancy and Kristy.

The two girls were unhurt, but Kristy was beginning to show the emotional strain of the day.

"She needs some rest," Nancy said softly. "Let's get to Igles."

The young sleuths guided their cars onto the road and drove to their hotel without further incident. A short time later, Kristy fell into an exhausted sleep in the room she shared with Nancy.

Turn to page 6.

The next morning, the two girls walked into the lodge's lobby with ice skates slung over their shoulders.

"I can't wait to get on the ice again!" Kristy exclaimed. "My leg muscles need to be loosened up."

She and Nancy headed for a small skating pond near the hotel, but as they walked toward the door, a clerk rushed up behind them.

"Miss Drew," he called out. "There's a telephone call for you. The man on the line said it's urgent!"

Nancy turned to her friend. "Kristy, please wait for me. I don't think you should be alone after what happened last night."

The young skater nodded impatiently as the titian-haired detective followed the clerk into the manager's office.

"I'm afraid your caller had to hang up," the man behind the desk told her. "He said he'd ring again in a few minutes."

Nancy sighed with frustration and sat down to wait, wondering what the urgent news might be. Ten minutes passed. Then the telephone rang shrilly.

Turn to page 7.

"Hello, this is Nancy Drew," the young sleuth said after she picked up the receiver. There was a click on the other end and the line went dead.

"What a nuisance!" Nancy said angrily. She asked the manager to take any messages for her and then went back to the lobby, where she ran into Frank and Joe Hardy.

"Morning, Nancy," Frank called out. "Where's the champion skater?"

"She's waiting for me at the door," Nancy replied. Then she gasped. Her friend was nowhere to be seen!

"Oh, no!" Nancy exclaimed. "I'm afraid she's gone on to the pond without me. We'd better hurry to find her. I just received a telephone call but the person hung up on me. It may have been a trick to separate us."

The three young detectives set off down a narrow path that had a splendid view of the towering, snow-capped mountains around Innsbruck. Within a short time, they came to the small pond, where they expected to find Kristy.

"The place is deserted!" Joe said, worriedly. "Even Kristy's boots are gone!"

"Look over there." Nancy pointed to the far bank of the pond, where the snow was marked up.

Turn to page 8.

The sleuths ran across the ice and bent down to study the footprints that led to a spot where a snowmobile had been parked. Its tracks traveled up a hill away from Igles.

Frank picked up a blue wool scarf. "It's Kristy's!" he cried out.

"She's been here," Nancy said anxiously. "I'm afraid she may be in trouble."

"We have to start looking for her," Frank urged. "Let's get back to the hotel and rent a snowmobile to follow those tracks."

"You two go," Nancy said. "I want to search the pond for more clues. Then I'll alert the police. I'm worried that Kristy may have been kidnapped!"

If you want to follow Frank and Joe on the snowmobile, turn to page 9.
If you want to stay with Nancy to investigate the pond for clues, turn to page 10.

The Hardys sprinted the distance back to the lodge. As they ran into the manager's office, Joe shouted out, "We need a snowmobile right away. Kristy Anderson may have been kidnapped!"

The manager jumped up from behind his desk and pulled a set of keys out of his pocket. "Here, take mine. It's the green one parked out in front." He added in a distressed voice, "I sure hope you find her."

Frank grabbed the keys and rushed outside, followed by his younger brother. They hopped on the green snowmobile and roared off to the pond. There, they passed Nancy Drew, who was still looking for clues.

"Good luck," she shouted as they roared by.

Frank circled around the pond to where the tracks of the other snowmobile began. Then he guided the vehicle into the lines cut into the snow.

"We've never trailed anybody like this before!" Joe yelled out from behind.

"It would be fun," Frank shouted back, "if Kristy wasn't in trouble."

The two detectives rode over rolling, snow-covered hills as they followed the tracks. Frank kept his eyes steadily on the path.

Suddenly, Joe hollered, "Hold it. I see something."

Turn to page 11.

As the Hardys rushed off to rent a snowmobile, Nancy studied the prints in the snow. From the narrow blade marks she saw, she deduced that Kristy had changed into her skates. The young sleuth walked onto the ice. Cut into its glistening surface was a perfect figure eight. As Nancy's eyes swept across the figure, she discerned some crude scratches in one of its loops.

She stooped down to study the marks. On closer examination, she saw that they were actually three letters.

"L-E-R," Nancy read aloud. "Kristy must have scratched that out with the tip of her skate blade. She was trying to tell us something before she was taken away. I wonder what it means?"

After a quick investigation of other parts of the pond, the blond sleuth hurried back to the lodge. She went directly to the manager's office to use the telephone.

"Connect me with the police in Innsbruck, please," she told the operator. When the local authorities came on the line she informed them of the circumstances surrounding Kristy's disappearance. The police chief assured her they would do everything possible to assist in finding the skater.

Turn to page 13.

His brother braked to a stop. Joe ran several yards back, then stooped down and picked something up. It was a red skate guard with "K. Anderson" embossed on it.

"It's Kristy's," he yelled as he ran back to the snowmobile. "Maybe she dropped it accidentally. Or," he added, "perhaps she left it as a clue."

"Keep your eyes peeled for anything else," Frank instructed after Joe had jumped on again. Then he stepped on the accelerator and shot forward.

A short time later, the tracks ahead of them merged onto a heavily trafficked road.

"It goes to the cable car," Joe said and pointed to the aerial tramway that climbed up a nearby mountain. "Maybe Kristy's abductor took her up there."

"You might be right," Frank answered. "But look at those tracks cutting off the road up ahead. They could have been made by the guy we're chasing."

If you think the two brothers should drive to the cable car, turn to page 12.

If you think they should follow the set of tracks, turn to page 15.

If you think the Hardys should call the police, turn to page 30.

"Let's try the cable car," Frank said after considering the situation. "We can ask the operators if they saw Kristy."

He steered their snowmobile down the road to the aerial tramway. They left the vehicle in a parking place and walked to where passengers bought tickets for the ride up the mountain.

"Excuse me," Frank said to the ticket seller. "We're looking for a friend of ours. She's eighteen years old, has blond hair and blue eyes. She might have been with a blond, blue-eyed man. Do you remember seeing them in the last fifteen minutes?"

The man shrugged. "Many girls have blond hair and blue eyes. Maybe your friend was here, maybe not."

"We'll buy two tickets," Frank said, giving up hope of getting information from the man.

As they walked toward the tramway, Joe suddenly rushed ahead to pick something up from the snow.

"Look at this!" he exclaimed, holding up Kristy's other skate guard. "Now we know she went up there."

Turn to page 25.

Next, Nancy dialed the number of Kristy's coach, Eric Schreiber, who was staying at a hotel in Innsbruck.

"Hello Eric," she said. "This is Nancy Drew. Please come to Igles at once. Kristy may have been kidnapped!"

"What?" he cried.

Nancy explained the events of the morning to the worried coach, then hung up and turned to the manager.

"Could you lend me a map of this area?" she asked. "I need to know what roads lead away from Igles and where they go."

"Of course," the manager replied.

Nancy took the map he gave her and spread it out on a table in the lobby. She studied the geographical features of the Tyrolean region. As she inspected each road and train route crisscrossing the mountains, her eyes fell upon the name of a small village northwest of Innsbruck.

"Lermoos!" she murmured. "L-E-R. Those three letters might just be a coincidence. Or they could be a clue Kristy left in the ice."

She went to her room and changed out of her skating outfit. Half an hour later there was an insistent knock on the door.

"Come in," Nancy called out.

Turn to page 14.

Eric Schreiber entered the room, an anxious look on his handsome face.

"Have you heard anything?" he asked.

"No, but I think Kristy left us a clue as she was kidnapped," Nancy replied. "She scratched the letters L-E-R in the ice. Do you have any idea what they might stand for?"

"L-E-R," the young man repeated as he paced back and forth in the room. "They don't mean anything to me."

"Did Kristy know of a place, or a person, whose name began with those letters?" the sleuth asked. "It's very important that we come up with the answer, Eric."

The coach stared out a window, deep in thought. Suddenly, he turned around to face Nancy.

"Leroux!" he announced. "Kristy knows a French skater named Jacques Leroux. He became quite emotionally involved with her, as a matter of fact. The relationship was all one-sided, though. Kristy told me that Leroux was a little unbalanced. She tried to avoid seeing him, even though he followed her around at skating competitions."

"Does he have blue eyes and blond hair?" Nancy asked excitedly, remembering the man in Kristy's dressing room.

"Why yes, but that's not so unusual around here," Eric replied.

Turn to page 17.

Frank turned the steering wheel to the left, trailing the set of tracks that cut sharply down a steep hill.

"Hey, there's another skate guard!" Joe shouted. "Up ahead."

Frank braked beside the red object in the snow and picked it up. It also had Kristy's name embossed on it.

"Now we know we're on the right track," Joe said. "Let's go."

Frank guided the snowmobile down the hill, which sloped into a frozen river. The trail they were following became invisible on the ice.

"This looks dangerous," Joe cautioned. "We've got a lot of weight on this machine."

"Kristy's abductor made it across," Frank said, pointing to a set of tracks on the bank across the river.

Suddenly Joe gasped. "Frank, do you see what I see?"

Turn to page 16.

Frank turned to look at a skater speeding toward them from behind a small island in the river. "It's Kristy!" he exclaimed.

The blond girl came to a fast stop beside the sleuths, throwing out pieces of ice with the tips of her blades.

"I escaped!" she panted. "When we came to the river, he was afraid the ice would not be strong enough for us to cross. While he stopped to figure out what to do, I managed to get away from him onto the ice. He was afraid to follow me with the snowmobile, and he didn't stand a chance to catch me on foot because I still had my skates on."

"Great!" Frank said. "Now tell us what happened."

"A blond man with really eerie blue eyes grabbed me at the skating pond. He asked where my gold medal was. I wouldn't tell him that I had it around my neck, under my sweater."

"But did he get it from you?" Joe asked.

"Yes," Kristy answered. "After he took me away from the pond, he threatened me—so I gave it to him."

"Why would anybody go to all that trouble for a skating medal?" Frank murmured. "Unless . . ."

"Unless what?" Kristy asked.

"That's what we have to find out," the dark-haired sleuth answered. "But first, let's get you back to Igles."

Turn to page 19.

A moment later, Frank and Joe Hardy walked into the room with downcast expressions on their faces.

Nancy quickly introduced the brothers to Eric Schreiber.

"We lost the trail of the snowmobile," Frank announced in a frustrated voice. "The tracks we were following merged into a busy road. It was impossible to sort them out at that point."

"Well, there's still hope," Nancy spoke up. "Kristy left us a clue." She described the letters the skater had scratched in the ice.

"But what does it mean?" Joe asked.

"I don't know for sure," the titian-haired sleuth replied, "but I'm working on two possibilities."

She walked over to the map of Austria, which she had spread open on the desk.

"First, there is a village named Lermoos not far from Innsbruck," she said, pointing it out to the Hardys. "Second, Eric recalls the name of Jacques Leroux. He's a French skater who has been following Kristy around."

"Sounds good, Nancy," Joe said with admiration.

"Let's get started then," the young sleuth suggested.

If you want to follow the detectives as they investigate Lermoos, turn to page 18.
If you want to follow their investigation of Jacques Leroux, turn to page 24.

Frank inspected the map of Austria more carefully.

"The road we followed the snowmobile tracks to goes in the direction of Lermoos," he said. "If we drive there, maybe we can find a lead to Kristy's whereabouts."

"I'll stay here," Eric volunteered, "and keep in touch with the police."

"Let's get going, then," Joe said urgently.

The three sleuths hurried from the room, taking the map along with them. They got into Nancy's red Volkswagen and drove to the small village of Lermoos.

During the journey, they discussed the clues they had to work on.

"We have to watch for a yellow snowmobile with black stripes," Nancy said. "That close call we had on the road last night may have been a kidnap attempt."

"The driver could have been the man we saw in Kristy's dressing room," Frank added.

Some time later, the young detectives arrived at a tiny village nestled at the foot of a spectacular, snow-covered mountain. A sign at its outskirts read LER-MOOS.

Turn to page 21.

Nancy was waiting at the lodge when the trio arrived, and the four friends talked about the events of the morning.

"I want to find out more about that medal," Frank said thoughtfully. "I'm going down to call the officials of last night's competition. They'll know where it came from."

As he left the room, Nancy worked up a sketch of the man she had seen in Kristy's dressing room. "Does this look like your abductor?" she asked the skater when she was finished.

"That's him all right," the girl replied with a shudder.

"We'll drop this off at the main police station in Innsbruck," Nancy decided. "They can send copies to the authorities throughout the country."

"You'll get your medal back, Kristy," Joe said reassuringly. "That guy won't get away with this."

At that moment, Frank burst into the room again.

"I found out who made the medal," he announced. "He's an old man in Innsbruck who is one of Austria's best goldsmiths."

Turn to page 20.

"Let's all go to Innsbruck," Nancy suggested. "Kristy, we'll drop you off at your coach's hotel where you'll be safe. I'll take my sketch to the police."

"And I want to check out that goldsmith's shop," Frank added eagerly.

The four young Americans piled into the white sedan with Joe at the wheel. He first drove to the hotel where Kristy's coach, Eric Schreiber, was staying, and delivered the skater safely into his care. Then Nancy made a quick stop at the central police station to drop off her sketch.

Finally, they were on their way to Bauerstrasse, where the goldsmith had his shop.

"There it is," Frank said and pointed to a second-floor window on the quiet side street. The name HANS BECKER was spelled out in gold letters on the glass pane.

Turn to page 38.

"There's not much here," Frank observed as they passed a cluster of chalet-type houses.

"Turn left," Nancy said from the back seat. "I see a sign for a restaurant."

When Frank pulled into the restaurant's parking lot, a black Mercedes was backing out. Its driver, a man in dark sunglasses and a fur hat, accelerated quickly, spinning the car around dangerously. Frank swerved to the side of the road to avoid a collision. The Mercedes shot by, heading up a narrow mountain road.

"A German," Joe observed, looking at the license plate. "I heard they drive fast there, but that was ridiculous!"

After parking the car, the companions walked into the restaurant, hoping to question someone about Kristy.

A ruddy-complected, middle-aged man was sitting behind the cash register near the door.

"Do you speak English?" Frank asked him.

Turn to page 22.

"Of course," the Austrian answered quickly. "Many English and American tourists come to my café."

"We're looking for a friend of ours," Frank continued. "A young American girl, with blond hair and blue eyes, very pretty."

"There are many pretty American girls around here," the man replied, looking at Nancy. "But this is the first one I've seen today."

"Have you noticed any strangers in the village lately, acting suspiciously?" Nancy asked, amused by his compliment.

"The American who just left the café came to Lermoos only yesterday," the Austrian said. "He doesn't seem like the type who enjoys winter sports."

"Do you mean the man in the black Mercedes?" Frank questioned. "We thought he was German."

"No, no, he is definitely American," the restaurant manager insisted. "He rented a chalet up the hill."

"Thank you for the information," Nancy said politely as the three sleuths left the café.

Outside, Frank excitedly hurried for the car. "I want to go after that Mercedes!" he said.

"Hold on," Joe called out. Look over there!"

Frank and Nancy glanced in the direction he was pointing. They saw a yellow snowmobile with black stripes zooming up another mountain road.

If you think the sleuths should pursue the black Mercedes, turn to page 61.

If you think they should chase the snowmobile, turn to page 80.

"We must find out whether Jacques Leroux has been in Innsbruck," Nancy said. "I'll telephone the police. They can do a quick canvass of all the hotels and pensiones in the area."

"I know one of the French skating coaches," Eric volunteered. "He may have seen Leroux at the competition last night."

The Hardys followed Nancy and the coach downstairs to the manager's office to make their calls. The authorities promised to investigate the registers of all the lodging places in and around Innsbruck. Eric's French acquaintance confirmed their suspicion that Jacques Leroux had been in the audience at the ice arena the previous evening.

"If it was Leroux who kidnapped Kristy," Nancy mused, "he may take her to a hiding place nearby. Or perhaps he will try to leave the country with her!"

"Remember that he has emotional problems," Eric added. "He may be totally unpredictable."

A short time later, a call for Nancy came from the police. After the young sleuth had finished speaking, she relayed the report to Frank, Joe, and Eric.

Turn to page 26.

The Hardys walked into one of the large cable cars that transported sightseers and skiers up the hill. They peered intently out the window as they began their ascent, checking out the ski trails and other paths on the mountain.

"There's the bobsled run that was built for the Innsbruck Olympics," Joe remarked, pointing out a window to the right.

"I wonder what else is on top of this mountain?" Frank mused. "It's a good thing we wore our heavy boots. We may be doing some climbing."

The cable car screeched to a stop at the station near the summit. The skiers piled out to the right where a trail zigzagged downward. To the left was a cafeteria and lookout point.

Frank and Joe searched the restaurant for Kristy, but without luck. Then they went outside where several skiers were taking a break.

"Where does this path lead to?" Frank asked them, pointing to a narrow trail that wound to the left.

"A lot of people walk it in the summer," one skier answered. "It's pretty treacherous now, but it's the only trail to go on foot from here."

"Let's take it," Joe said.

Turn to page 28.

"Jacques Leroux was staying at the Tyroler Pensione in Innsbruck until this morning. He registered his address as 182 Rue de Marchant, Paris. The clerk at the pensione remembers that when Leroux checked out this morning, he was holding two rail tickets.

"One for himself," Joe speculated, ". . . and one for Kristy!"

"But how could he take Kristy on a train?" Frank questioned. "Wouldn't she try to escape?"

"He may have threatened her," Nancy answered. "If he was the driver of that snowmobile we met on the road last night, he's capable of dangerous behavior. We'd better get to the railway station as soon as possible!"

Turn to page 27.

The three young detectives jumped into their rented sedan and quickly drove to the Innsbruck train station. They parked the car and ran inside. The rumbling of a departing train filled their ears as they rushed through the lobby to the platform area.

"Where's that train going?" Frank asked a conductor in a blue uniform.

"To Zurich, Switzerland," the man replied.

"Did you happen to see a young man and woman, both blond, board the train?" Nancy asked.

"Why, yes, I did. I noticed the girl because she seemed terribly nervous. They had tickets to Gare de l'Est in Paris. You see, there's a connecting train from Zurich—"

"We have to catch that train!" Frank muttered.

"It's a bit late now, brother," Joe said.

"An express will be coming through in half an hour," the official informed them. "It could get you to Zurich just in time to catch the connecting train before it departs for Paris."

"That sounds pretty risky to me," Frank responded. "Maybe we should fly to Paris and be at the station when the train comes in."

If you think the detectives should take the next express train, turn to page 31.
If you think they should fly to Paris, turn to page 41.

The young detectives set out on the path, which followed a ridge in the mountain. Joe led the way, walking quickly over the hard-packed snow. Suddenly, he lost his foothold and began to slip.

"Hey, be careful," Frank yelled, grabbing his brother's arm and pulling him back onto the path.

"Looks like this is where most people stop," Joe observed, noticing that the footprints on the path were thinning out.

"You're right," Frank added, "but somebody went on recently." He pointed to two fresh sets of prints, one large and one small, that continued along the ridge.

"Those could be Kristy's," Joe said excitedly. "Come on!"

The brothers followed the trail along the slippery path for fifteen minutes. Finally, they saw a small mountain hostel ahead of them.

"I'll bet she's in there," the younger Hardy said. "But I wonder who's with her!"

Turn to page 29.

The sleuths crept up to the hostel, which huddled against a jagged cliff.

"We don't have any cover," Frank warned. "If anyone's looking out a window, we'll be seen for sure."

"Let's just play it by ear," Joe replied, walking up to the door. He rapped on the hard wood several times, and shortly a husky man in ski clothes opened the door.

"What do you want?" he asked gruffly.

The detectives peered over his shoulder into the room. They saw Kristy sitting by a fireplace with two other men!

"Hey, grab those guys," one of them yelled as soon as he saw the Hardys.

The husky man lunged for them. Still Frank and Joe hesitated. They knew they should run. But if they did, Kristy would be all alone and in danger!

If you think Frank and Joe should stay with Kristy, turn to page 33.

If you think they should try to escape, turn to page 34.

"Since we're not sure, we'd better call the police," Frank decided. "Let's get back to the hotel."

The older Hardy revved the engine of the snowmobile and headed toward Igles. When they arrived, he parked the small vehicle in front of the lodge and rushed into the manager's office.

"Here are your keys," Frank said to the man. "We lost the kidnapper's trail and I need to call the police."

The manager pointed to the telephone, and Frank quickly dialed the central police station. He explained in detail how they had followed the snowmobile's trail to a road near the cable car.

After he had finished his conversation, he turned to Joe and said, "Two detectives are on their way up with several officers. We can join them when they arrive. Right now, I want to check in with Nancy."

Turn to page 36.

Thirty minutes later, the young detectives boarded the express train to Zurich, Switzerland. Nancy and Joe slipped into two adjoining seats and Frank sat down across from them. The train pulled out of the station exactly on schedule, beginning its four-hour journey.

The sleuths tried to relax and enjoy the stunning mountain scenery outside their window. But all three were preoccupied by thoughts about their young friend.

"Kristy has a level head on her shoulders," Joe said reassuringly to the others. "She won't try anything foolish."

"Let's just make sure we don't waste any time when we arrive in Zurich," Frank said as he studied the train schedule. "We have to run to platform sixteen as fast as possible if we want to catch their Paris-bound train."

The detectives spent the rest of the trip carefully planning their strategy to rescue Kristy from the dangerous Jacques Leroux.

Turn to page 32.

When the train wheels screeched to a stop at the station in Zurich, Nancy, Frank, and Joe leapt onto the platform. Joe immediately asked a railworker for the fastest route to platform sixteen. Then the sleuths took off toward the Paris-bound train. They came up to it just as an attendant was slamming shut the doors of each car. They jumped into the last one with barely seconds to spare. Before they could catch their breath, the express began to pull out of the station.

"We made it!" Joe gasped.

"Let's just hope that Kristy is on this train," Nancy added anxiously, "—somewhere."

The young detectives began to carry out the plan they had agreed on during the trip from Innsbruck. They walked down the aisle, carefully inspecting the people in each seat. As they came to the end, Frank pulled open the sliding door that opened to a short passageway between the last car and the next one.

"Hey, this is exciting," Joe said as he listened to the loud rumbling of the wheels on the track.

"It'll get more exciting when we find Leroux!" Frank added, stepping into the adjoining car.

Turn to page 58.

Frank couldn't pull his eyes away from the girl's frightened face. He grabbed Joe's arm. "We have to see if she's okay," he whispered.

Their husky assailant roughly shoved the Hardys into the small hostel. When they walked over to Kristy, they recognized the man with the icy blue eyes, who was sitting on her right.

Kristy looked at her two friends gratefully. "I'm sorry I've gotten you into trouble," she said softly. "But I'm so glad you're here!"

"Max, are these Hardy's sons?" the man beside Kristy asked his blond-haired partner.

"They're Frank and Joe Hardy," Max answered in a sinister voice. "And they walked right into our clutches, boss."

"Well, well, well," the leader of the kidnappers said with a satisfied smirk. "Won't Fenton Hardy be interested to hear about this."

Joe threw a worried look at his brother. "What's all this have to do with our father?" he demanded.

Turn to page 35.

"Run, Frank!" Joe yelled finally, "We've got to get help!"

The two Hardys took off away from the cabin, just escaping the clutches of their husky assailant.

As they hurried toward the path that led to the cable car, they heard footsteps pounding through the snow behind them. Joe looked back and saw the husky man and a blond accomplice desperately chasing them.

"They're coming fast, Frank," the young sleuth called to his brother ahead of him. "Watch your footing."

A second later, Joe himself slipped on the treacherous path and sprawled out on the snow. The blond kidnapper behind was too close to avoid a collision. He tripped over Joe and went hurtling over the edge of the cliff. With a scream of pain, he landed in a snowbank ten feet below.

Frank whirled around and jumped over his brother at the husky assailant, who had stopped to gaze down at his partner. The dark-haired detective caught the man off guard and threw him to the ground. Joe picked himself up and went to Frank's aid.

Turn to page 57.

"Your father is causing us a lot of trouble in Geneva," the boss snarled, "with his investigation. We took Miss Anderson as a hostage to . . . let's say . . . discourage the American government from backing your father anymore. But now he'll have his sons to worry about. It's all very simple, you see. He'll have to trade his silence for your safety."

Max got up and pushed the young detectives onto the bench beside Kristy. "You stay there," he commanded. Then he added, "Boss, let's make sure no one is following them."

The two men walked out of the hostel to search the mountain path while their husky confederate stood guard at the door. No one else seemed to be around.

"Wow," Joe said quietly, "this is a real mess!"

"Do you know what they plan to do with us?" Frank asked Kristy.

"I heard them say they'd wait until dark to leave here," the skater replied in a frightened voice. "Then, I don't know what will happen to us!"

"We can take care of that guy—" Joe began but Kristy interrupted him.

"Don't! I think he has a gun in his pocket!"

Turn to page 66.

As the Hardys walked into the room that Nancy and Kristy shared, they saw their friend sitting at a writing desk, staring out a window with a pensive expression on her face.

"Nancy, what's the matter?" Frank questioned. "You look like you've heard terrible news!"

The titian-blond detective put down a letter she had been reading. Then she said, "Please come in and shut the door. I don't want anybody else to know about this for a while."

Frank and Joe followed her request, then sat down on the edge of a bed.

"Is it about Kristy?" Frank asked.

"Yes," Nancy replied in a quivery voice. "I found this letter from her in the bottom of my suitcase. I don't think she expected me to notice it for a while."

The young sleuth unfolded the handwritten paper and began to read its contents aloud.

Turn to page 37.

Dear Nancy,

By the time you see this letter, I will be in another country—another world, really—with the man I love. You have seen Sergei Bornov skate and must understand why I want to marry him. We share a love of the ice that binds us together despite the differences between our countries. I wish you could be at our wedding, but since my parents would never agree to this, I think it's best if I slip away quietly. Sergei plans to meet me at the skating pond this morning. Good-bye, dear friend, and thank you.

　　　　　　　　　　　　　　　　　Kristy

As Nancy let the letter drop into her lap, Frank sighed.

"It's hard to believe, isn't it?" he said. "Are you sure the letter is genuine?"

"I'm sure," Nancy replied. "I know her handwriting."

"What will we tell the police?" Joe asked. "They'll be here any minute."

Turn to page 60.

The three sleuths walked from their car to a street-level entrance that opened to a flight of stairs. They climbed up to the next floor and knocked on the door, which had a frosted glass window. There was no answer.

Frank tried the knob, but it wouldn't turn. "I guess we're out of luck," he said, disappointed.

At that moment, the detectives heard a loud groan in the shop. Frank unsuccessfully tried to open the door again. Then there were more sounds of a struggle on the other side.

"Break the glass," Nancy suggested. "Somebody in there is in trouble!"

Frank shattered the window and reached through to push down the handle. Joe and Nancy entered the shop first. They spied a back room, rushed toward it, and flung open the door. At the far end of the room stood a blond man holding a knife over an older man. When the assailant saw the young detectives, he ran to an open window and scrambled out.

Turn to page 40.

"Come on, Frank," Joe called to his brother behind him. "Let's go after him."

The Hardys climbed through the window in pursuit of the attacker.

Nancy looked at the white-faced older man, who was trembling with fear.

"Mr. Becker?" she asked.

The man nodded weakly.

"What was that man doing here?" the sleuth inquired.

If you want to stay with Nancy, turn to page 43.
If you want to follow Frank and Joe, turn to page 46.

After carefully studying a rail schedule, the sleuths decided it was too chancy to try to catch the train Kristy and Leroux were on.

"Let's notify the police about our lead," Nancy suggested, "and then go to the airport. We'll catch the first plane out with a connection to Paris."

After calling the authorities, she joined Frank and Joe in their car, and they drove to the airport. On the way, Joe checked the train schedule he had brought along for the arrival time of the Paris train.

"Kristy and Leroux will get to the Gare de l'Est at nine-thirty tonight," he said. "That gives us plenty of time to stake out the station."

As soon as they parked their sedan, the young detectives rushed to the departure area of the airport. Frank inquired about flights at the information desk and learned that they could land in Paris at seven o'clock.

Turn to page 42.

Three hours later, Nancy, Frank, and Joe were gazing at the snow-covered peaks of the Austrian and Swiss Alps. They admired the magnificent scenery, but their thoughts were still on Kristy.

"She's down there somewhere," Nancy murmured, "with that crazy Jacques Leroux."

"I wonder what he plans to do with her?" Frank speculated with a worried look on his face. "He loved her once, but they say hate is the other side of the coin."

"Don't worry so much," Joe reassured them. "We'll catch Leroux."

The plane began its descent into Zurich, Switzerland, where there was a delay of several hours before the sleuths could board a plane ·to France. They passed the time on the ground discussing their plan of action at the Paris rail station. Soon, they were airborne again, flying northwest to the French capital.

"We're right on schedule," Frank said, checking his watch. "Our landing time will be in one and a half hours."

Nancy picked up the newspaper tucked into the pocket of the seat in front of her. As she read the headline, a frustrated look came over her face.

"Oh, no," she groaned. "The French air controllers are involved in a job dispute. They plan a slowdown at all airports today!"

Turn to page 49.

"He tried to kill me," Mr. Becker whispered. "But perhaps I deserve to die. I've done something terrible."

Nancy stared at the man curiously.

"Call the police, young lady, whoever you are," he went on. "They're the only ones who can protect me now."

Nancy followed the man's request, explaining to the chief what had happened. While they waited for the authorities to arrive, Mr. Becker went to his desk and gathered papers together.

"It's all over now," he muttered under his breath. "It's all over."

"Mr. Becker," the sleuth asked cautiously, "does this have something to do with the gold skating medal?"

The goldsmith looked at her in surprise.

"How did you know?" he queried.

"I'm a friend of Kristy Anderson's," Nancy explained. "Her medal was stolen, and I'm trying to get it back."

"She never should have won it in the first place!" the man exclaimed. "Everyone thought another skater would win. My contacts were certain the medal would go to their country."

"Your contacts?" Nancy questioned.

Turn to page 62.

Just then, the cable car started to move down the hill again. The kidnappers turned around to face their three captives, and Joe realized his escape plan was ruined.

The car came to a sudden halt at the station, and Max roughly pushed the young Americans out onto the platform.

Then he and the leader went to talk to the operator, leaving the husky man to guard the prisoners. He had his hand in his pocket on a bulging object, which he wanted the young people to believe was a gun. But Frank had observed him closely and felt the man was only bluffing. The young detective decided to take a chance.

He whispered to Kristy and Joe, "Let's try to make a getaway. Kristy, you point up at the mountain and let out a scream. Joe, you grab Kristy and run off to the left. I'll take off to the right. That should confuse him."

"Now?" Kristy asked as she stared at the husky man standing nearby.

"Now!" Frank said softly.

Kristy turned and stared uphill. Then she let out a blood-curdling scream. The husky man looked up and searched the mountain.

A second later, Joe, Kristy, and Frank fled in two different directions!

If you want to follow Joe and Kristy, turn to page 45.
If you want to follow Frank, turn to page 48.

Joe held Kristy's arm tightly and pulled her through the snow away from the cable-car station. He headed toward the small café that served skiers during the day.

He threw a quick backward glance over his shoulder and saw Max headed in their direction.

"Come on, Kristy, we've got to get away!" he whispered urgently.

As the two reached the café, they ran around to its back. Suddenly, they stopped dead in their tracks.

"Dad!" Joe said in amazement. "Am I glad to see you!"

Fenton Hardy was crouched behind the building with four detectives from the Innsbruck police.

"Nancy called me in Geneva to report that you were missing," he quickly explained. "I flew here early tonight. The police followed your trail to the cable car. We've been waiting for you to come down the mountain." Then the investigator asked worriedly, "Where's Frank?"

"He ran off in the opposite direction," Joe said. "You'd better catch these crooks before they get away!"

Turn to page 50.

The assailant had climbed out of the window and jumped onto a truck that was parked right below it. When he heard the boys coming after him, he threw them a quick backward glance.

"It's him!" Joe exclaimed. "It's Kristy's abductor!"

"We can't lose him now!" Frank said grimly. "Come on, jump!"

Both boys landed on the truck. The blond man had already vaulted over the side and to the ground and was running along the street.

"I'll get the car," Frank yelled. "You follow him."

The brothers split off in two directions. Joe sprinted after the assailant, keeping a steady watch on his green ski jacket. The man ran to the front of the shop and then down Bauerstrasse. Suddenly, he slipped from Joe's view into an alley.

The boy hurried to the narrow street. Just as he reached it, he saw the assailant pull away in a brown van.

"Come on, Frank, where are you?" Joe muttered nervously as the vehicle disappeared around a corner.

Turn to page 47.

Just then, he heard the screech of brakes behind him. He turned around to see Frank in their white sedan.

Joe jumped into the front seat and directed his brother into the alleyway after the van. They caught sight of it driving down a main street to the right.

"I'll watch the traffic. You keep your eyes on the van," Frank suggested.

Joe called out directions as they zigzagged through the city after the van.

"He seems to be headed north," Joe guessed.

The detectives continued to trail the man to the base of a steep mountain.

"How's he going to get up there?" Frank wondered.

"Look, there's a cog railway," his brother pointed out. "He stopped right next to it."

Just then, Frank had to brake to a quick halt when a large tour bus pulled across the road in front of them and stopped to let off passengers.

"Drat!" he exclaimed. "I can't see a thing!"

Turn to page 72.

Frank sprinted with all his might to the parking lot, where he had left the green snowmobile. He pulled the keys from his pocket, and jumped on the vehicle, and turned the ignition key. The next moment he shot off into the dark. The husky kidnapper who had been pursuing him let out an angry yell when he saw the detective roar away.

Frank turned on the high-beam light, searching the road for his brother and Kristy. Minutes later, he saw them running toward him. He braked quickly and waited as the two squeezed into the seat behind him. They sped away just as Max reached the road.

"We've got to call the police!" Frank shouted as he steered the vehicle along the snow-packed surface.

A short time later, they came to a lodge on the outskirts of Igles. Frank stopped in front and turned off the engine. Then the three young Americans ran inside, exhausted but safe.

Frank immediately called the local authorities and reported the kidnappers. The police chief said he would send several cars to pursue the criminals.

Turn to page 52.

An hour later, an announcement over the plane's intercom confirmed the detectives' fears. The pilot informed the passengers that landing would be delayed until approximately 8:45.

Frank pulled out a detailed map of Paris that he had purchased at the airport.

"We're in real trouble now," he said, tracing the route from the airport to the train station. "A taxi might be able to get to Gare de l'Est in time, and it might not!"

As their plane began to circle over the French capital, waiting for clearance to land, the sleuths devised a new strategy.

"I'll go on to Rue de Marchant," Nancy suggested, "the address that Leroux gave at the pensione. If you miss Kristy and him at the train station, I'll be waiting for them there."

"Okay," Frank agreed. "Joe and I will make a dash for the station as soon as we get our feet on the ground."

The minutes stretched into what seemed hours as the plane continued to circle Paris. Finally, the captain announced that he could land.

As the jet taxied to its stop, Frank and Joe anxiously waited for the seat-belt sign to go off. As soon as it did, they jumped into action.

"It's getting close," Joe said nervously as he moved for the door. "I hope we make it!"

If you want to follow Frank and Joe, turn to page 53.
If you want to follow Nancy, turn to page 56.

Mr. Hardy and the detectives rushed out from their hiding place and quickly apprehended Max, who ran right into them. Then they headed for the lift station where the leader of the kidnappers was standing with the cable-car operator. The police caught the two men before they had a chance to escape.

A moment later, Fenton Hardy ran into the darkness to find Frank. He discovered his older son wrestling the third kidnapper to the ground, and helped him bring the last criminal to the station, where the police handcuffed him with his accomplices.

When the crooks had been taken away, Frank asked his father, "What were those guys up to, Dad? They said you were interfering with their plans."

"They're hired terrorists," Fenton Hardy explained. "I was called in to investigate their activities at the United Nations headquarters in Geneva. They hoped to create an international incident by planting a bomb in the offices there."

"But why did they kidnap me?" Kristy asked.

"They hoped to sidetrack my investigation by holding you for ransom. They knew the American government would be very concerned about your safety," Fenton Hardy told the young skater.

Turn to page 51.

Just then, Nancy Drew arrived on the scene.

"Kristy, are you all right?" she cried out.

Her friend nodded with a grateful smile. "I wouldn't be if it hadn't been for all of you. How can I ever thank you?"

"How about getting us tickets to the next Winter Olympics?" Joe suggested. "We'd like to see you win another gold medal!"

END

Later that night, Frank, Joe, and Kristy sat in the girls' hotel room, telling the young sleuth the story of their adventure.

"When we telephoned Dad in Geneva after we got back," Joe explained, "he said our kidnappers were hired terrorists. They were planning to assassinate a famous diplomat at the United Nations headquarters."

"Wow!" the titian-blond sleuth exclaimed. "You were dealing with really dangerous characters."

"They won't be dangerous anymore," Frank said. "The police chief called to say that they've been apprehended. They'll probably spend the rest of their lives in prison."

Turn to page 55.

Frank and Joe ran into the Paris airport and luckily passed through customs quickly.

"Gare de l'Est," the older Hardy shouted to a taxi driver outside the airport, "as quickly as possible!"

The driver nodded his head, and the Hardys jumped into the back of his white Peugeot. The taxi shot off into the evening traffic, weaving its way to the rail station at the north end of Paris.

Sometime later, Frank pointed excitedly to the large building they were approaching. "There it is, Joe. We've really got to move!" He handed the driver several francs and then leapt from the car with his brother close behind.

The Hardys rushed into the station, checked the large board that listed arrival platforms, and then headed for platform number twenty-four.

"It's nine thirty-two, Frank," Joe said worriedly as they came up to the platform. Passengers were already filing through the gate into the crowded terminal. Kristy and her abductor were nowhere to be seen.

Turn to page 54.

Just then, Frank caught sight of two blond heads emerging from the train.

"There they are," he whispered to his brother. "Get ready."

They watched as Leroux guided Kristy toward the exit, holding her arm tightly. The young skater looked exhausted and frightened. Suddenly, she spotted her friends in the crowd.

"Frank, Joe!" she called out desperately and tried to run toward them. But Leroux jerked her back and searched the crowd with his icy blue eyes. As his gaze fell upon the Hardys, a look of fear crossed his face. He pushed Kristy in front of him as they passed through the narrow gate. Then, when they were only a few yards from the Hardys, he shoved the skater roughly at the detectives.

Kristy fell into Frank's arms, sobbing. Leroux sped away through the crowd, making a clever escape.

"I'll get him," Joe yelled as he dashed off after the criminal.

Turn to page 89.

Kristy sighed with exhaustion and fell back on a bed.

"I'm beat!" she murmured. Then she caught a glimpse of a newspaper lying on the bedstand.

"Hey, that's me!" she exclaimed, looking at the picture on the front page. It showed her receiving her gold medal at the ice arena the night before.

"The internationally famous Kristy Anderson," Frank said, waving an arm toward the blond skater.

"Hey," Joe said with a broad smile. "I can't wait to see tomorrow's headlines. We'll all be internationally famous!"

END

Nancy hurried into the Paris airport. After going through customs, she stopped to buy a map of Paris. She located Rue de Marchant in the city's 11th arrondissement, which she knew was the students' quarter of the capital. Then she went outside to hail a taxi.

Half an hour later, Nancy stepped onto the pavement in front of Rue de Marchant. She glanced up at the old apartment house in which Leroux lived. Then she walked quickly to the corner, where she had seen a drugstore from the window of her taxi.

She purchased a large felt hat. After that, she went to a public telephone and dialed the Paris police. Speaking French, she carefully explained to the authorities who she was and why she had come to Paris. The police listened to her story and promised their help.

Turn to page 94.

"We don't have anything to tie this guy up with," Frank gasped with frustration as he wrestled against the strong man.

"I'll try to get his boot laces," Joe said. He pinned down the assailant's legs and undid the strong leather ties.

Several minutes later, the Hardys had the man's arms bound behind his back. Frank looked down the cliff at the blond kidnapper, who glared back at him with a painful grimace on his face.

"He's not going anywhere," the older Hardy commented. "Joe, take this guy to the cable-car station and call the police. I'll go get Kristy."

"Okay," his brother replied, "but be careful!"

If you want to go with Frank, turn to page 63.
If you want to stay with Joe, turn to page 83.

Nancy checked out the seats on the left side of the aisle while Joe inspected the passengers on the right. Frank followed a short distance behind in case Leroux tried to make an escape. But they traveled through the second and third cars without discovering Kristy and her abductor.

As they stepped through the sliding door into the fourth carriage, they noted that it was made of individual compartments, all located on the right side of the train.

"They might be in here," Frank whispered. "It's a better hiding place for Leroux."

The sleuths peered through the glass windows into each set of seats, searching for their friend. Halfway through the car, Nancy glanced into the next compartment and caught her breath. She was staring into the surprised eyes of Kristy Anderson!

Turn to page 59.

Silently, Nancy lifted her finger to her lips. Kristy softened her tense expression and dropped her gaze to the floor.

The titian-haired detective indicated to the Hardy brothers behind her that she had found Kristy.

Frank and Joe furtively walked past the window to glance at the seat opposite the skater. They met the icy blue stare of Jacques Leroux.

"Now!" Frank exclaimed to Joe. The brothers slid open the doors and lunged for the Frenchman. Meanwhile, Nancy reached an arm inside and pulled Kristy into the aisle.

Leroux struggled against the Hardys, but soon they had him pinned against the seat.

"You two find a conductor," Joe said to the girls, "while we'll make sure this guy doesn't get away."

Nancy and Kristy hurried into the next car where they explained to a conductor everything that had happened.

Turn to page 76.

"We'll have to say we were wrong about Kristy being kidnapped," Nancy answered.

"Okay, I'll take care of the police," Frank announced.

"I'm going to call my father right away," the titian-haired sleuth said. "He'll know the legal ins and outs of the situation. And he can contact Kristy's parents."

"Whew!" Joe said, still amazed by the news. "Kristy might be making a big mistake."

"I'm worried about her, too," Nancy replied. "But she's legally an adult. And she has the right to make her own decisions."

"I just hope she's happy," Frank remarked as he went out the door.

Nancy wiped a tear from her cheek and added, "And stays happy."

END

"The snowmobile can turn off the road any minute," Frank said. "Let's drive after the Mercedes. I watched it go up the hill to the west."

They hopped in their Volkswagen and the older Hardy started the engine. A moment later they took off up the winding mountain road that had markers pointing to a ski-lift station. The young detectives passed several vacation chalets on the way, but saw no sign of the black Mercedes.

"If we've lost him, we're back to square one," Nancy said with frustration.

Soon the sleuths came to the ski station, where a lift carried passengers to the top of the mountain.

"Let's stop here," Frank suggested. "Maybe someone has seen the driver of the Mercedes and knows where he's staying."

"Good idea," Nancy agreed. "I also want to check in with Eric to see if the police have uncovered any clues."

They parked their car near a building where ski equipment could be rented, then jumped out and hurried over to a small hut close to the lift.

Turn to page 64.

"My spy contacts," Mr. Becker said bitterly. Then he heard the sound of footsteps on the stairs and sighed. "My last breath of freedom," he remarked despairingly.

When the police chief entered the room, Mr. Becker sat down and spilled out his story. For years, he had been paid as a spy to send information to NATO adversaries. His profession as a goldsmith served as an excellent cover for his clandestine activities. He often passed his secrets by hiding them in code on jewelry or other gold pieces.

"Do you mean to say that Kristy's medal held spy information?" Nancy exclaimed.

"Yes," Mr. Becker answered, "but it ended up going to the wrong country. One of my contacts had to get it back. Once he had stolen the medal, he decided to get me out of the way because he didn't trust me any more and was afraid I'd talk. I'd be a dead man now if you hadn't walked in."

The police chief took Mr. Becker firmly by the arm. "We'll have to go to the station sir," he declared.

The captured spy stood up and turned to Nancy.

"Good-bye, young lady. I hope your friend gets her medal back."

"I'm sure she will," Nancy replied, her thoughts quickly turning to Frank and Joe.

Turn to page 93.

Frank dashed back to the cabin. He anxiously wondered what the third kidnapper was doing with Kristy. As he neared their hiding place, he saw the man, who was tall and dark-haired, standing on top of a steep, snow-covered hill with Kristy beside him. Both of them had downhill skis strapped to their feet.

The kidnapper started down the mountain, pulling the blond girl with him. Frank knew he couldn't follow on foot. He ran into the cabin and spied two more pairs of skis and boots. Hastily, he got himself ready for the pursuit.

Minutes later, he was skiing after Kristy and her captor.

Turn to page 110.

While Frank and Joe went to question the young Austrians working at the lift, Nancy ran to a phone booth and called the hotel.

"Hello, Eric, is that you?" she said when she got the coach on the line. "Is there any news of Kristy?"

A look of alarm passed over her face as she listened to Schreiber's report. When he was finished, she hung up the phone and rushed to Frank and Joe.

"Eric found a ransom note in my room in the lodge," she told them anxiously. "He doesn't know how it got there, but the kidnappers are demanding a hundred thousand dollars for Kristy's release!"

"What are the details?" Joe demanded immediately.

"They want the money in small denominations, unmarked bills," Nancy answered. "Eric is supposed to drop it off in a canvas bag at midnight."

"Where?" Frank asked urgently.

"That's the problem," the titian-haired sleuth answered. "They won't notify him about the drop-off place until eleven o'clock."

Turn to page 65.

"We have to find Kristy before then!" Joe exclaimed. "One guy who works here thinks he knows what chalet the Mercedes driver rented. It's a quarter of a mile up the hill."

"Let's check it out," Nancy replied.

As the three detectives went to the loading area, Frank glanced at the lift transporting people up the mountain.

"Hey, look at the fourth chair from the bottom," he called out.

Nancy and Joe followed his gaze to the single passenger perched on the slatted seat. It was a man wearing a fur hat and sunglasses! On his feet were a pair of cross-country skis.

"I'll rent skis and try to follow that guy," Frank decided. "You two call the police and tell them what we're up to. Then go back to the chalet for further news."

"Okay," Joe agreed as his brother hurried into the rental shop.

If you want to go with Nancy and Joe, turn to page 68.
If you want to go with Frank, turn to page 77.

The three hostages huddled around the fire, trying to keep warm as the long hours of their captivity passed. The three kidnappers kept a close watch on the Hardys, preventing any chance of escape.

As daylight faded from the sky, Joe realized he was starving.

"Hey, aren't you going to feed us?" he demanded.

"Not until we get out of here," Max answered roughly.

"Where are you taking us?" Frank asked, more eager for information than food.

"Somewhere your father will never find you," the leader replied with a smirk.

Several hours later, the captors ordered Frank, Joe, and Kristy to get to their feet. The young hostages were shoved out the door and along the mountain path in the direction of the cable-car station.

"Where are we going?" Joe whispered. "Everything is pitch black up here."

"I wish I knew," Frank said worriedly as he helped Kristy along the treacherous path.

At last, they reached the tramway stop.

"Get in," Max ordered as he pointed to a waiting car. "We're going down."

Turn to page 67.

The hostages and their three captors filed inside.

The leader of the kidnappers looked at his watch. "Okay, give the signal," he said to his husky assistant. The man pulled a high-beam flashlight from his jacket and directed a series of signals down the hill. A minute later, they began their eerie descent down the dark mountain.

Kristy moved near Frank.

"I'm scared," she murmured. He took her hand and held it tightly as the car swayed on its cable in the cold air.

"We're almost at the bottom," Joe said as he watched the dark shadow of the downhill station loom closer.

Just then, there was a wrenching screech, and their car came to a sudden halt.

Turn to page 71.

A short while later, Nancy slid behind the wheel of the Volkswagen with Joe beside her. The two drove away from the ski station along the mountain road. A quarter of a mile later, they spotted a small chalet tucked inside a stand of fir trees.

"Look, there's the Mercedes we saw down in Lermoos," Joe pointed out.

"Maybe that man on the lift wasn't the driver!" Nancy said. "We'd better check this place out." She pulled off the road a short distance from the house.

The two left the car and approached the chalet from the side, concealing themselves in the trees. As they circled around to the back, they heard a snow-mobile approaching. It came around the far side of the building and stopped at a rear door.

"This is it!" Joe whispered to Nancy as they stared at the yellow snowmobile with black stripes along its sides. The driver pulled off his dark bubble helmet as he walked toward the door. The sleuths caught a glimpse of his blond head before he disappeared inside.

"I wish Frank were here," Joe said. "There are at least two guys in there."

"But we've got to get Kristy out!" Nancy replied urgently.

Turn to page 69.

The two detectives crept closer for a better look, still staying concealed behind the fir trees.

"I can't believe it!" Joe whispered suddenly.

"What?"

"He left the keys in the snowmobile. Do you think you could drive it?"

"Sure," Nancy replied. "What's your plan?"

Joe pulled his ski cap down over his hair. Then he took a pair of goggles from his coat pocket and put them on.

"Maybe they won't recognize me," he said. "I'll go to the front and pretend I ran out of gas to distract the men in the house. You try to sneak in the back way and find Kristy. If you two can get out of the house, get on the snowmobile and take off."

"Okay," Nancy agreed. "But let's be careful."

She waited while Joe crept through the trees to the road. A few minutes later, she heard his knock on the front door of the house. Quickly, she dashed to the back door and pushed it open.

Turn to page 70.

She found herself in a small kitchen with a stairway leading to the second floor. Two men were talking in the front room.

"Who's that kid out there?" one asked.

"I don't know. Ignore him and maybe he'll go away," came the answer.

Nancy heard Joe pound on the door again. Then she quietly slipped up the stairs to the next floor. A faint sound came from behind a closed door. Cautiously, Nancy pushed the door open. Then she gasped. She was staring into the frightened eyes of her friend.

Kristy was lying on a bed, bound and gagged. Nancy rushed over to her, pulled a pocket knife out of her jacket, and cut the ropes. As she freed the skater's mouth, Kristy began to cry from relief. Quickly, Nancy motioned for her to be silent. The two girls crept to the door and went out into the hallway.

They heard Joe Hardy's voice downstairs.

"Listen, all I need is a little gas," he pleaded.

"You can get it at the ski station, kid," a gruff voice answered. "Now get out of here!"

Turn to page 105.

"What's the matter?" the leader shouted out. The three captors rushed to the side of the car with an open window. They yelled down to the operator in the station.

Meanwhile, Joe had been eyeing a small door labeled EMERGENCY EXIT. Stealthily, he elbowed his brother and pointed to it.

Frank immediately understood what Joe wanted to do. He shook his head firmly in disagreement. Even though they were not too far above ground at this point, he felt a jump was too dangerous.

If you think the escape attempt is too dangerous, turn to page 44.

If you think Joe should take the risk and try to escape, turn to page 78.

When the tour bus finally cleared the road, Frank pulled up beside the assailant's van. But the blond man was nowhere in sight.

Joe glanced up and saw the small funicular train beginning its journey up the mountain.

"He's on it," the boy said with dismay as he spotted the man's green jacket in one of the cars. "All we can do, I guess, is wait for the next trip."

The Hardys watched the small train climb the steep grade to a station halfway up the mountain. The blond assailant got off with the other passengers, then hurried down a path out of sight.

Meanwhile, the cog engine began its descent. As soon as it arrived at the bottom, Frank and Joe hopped into the first car. Several minutes later, the detectives began their slow journey up.

"This is great for sightseeing," Joe remarked, gazing at the panoramic view of Innsbruck below them. "But it's a terrible way to chase a crook!"

When the young detectives finally reached the station, they rushed down the path the assailant had taken.

"Where could he have gone from here?" Joe mused.

"There's your answer," Frank replied in an awed voice.

Turn to page 73.

Joe followed his brother's gaze to a rock ledge a quarter of a mile away. The man in the green jacket was standing on it, a red hang glider around his body. With a breathtaking leap, he soared out from the mountain.

The brothers rushed to the spot from where the fugitive had taken off. Two young men were running up from a hut on the other side, watching the hang glider float like a huge butterfly in the air. Another glider was set up on the ground nearby.

Turn to page 75.

"That guy stole my wings," one of the men complained angrily in an American accent.

"That's not all he's stolen," Frank said.

Joe walked over to the second glider. It was similar to the one he had used in the mountains of New England.

"I'll get your glider back," he said to the American, "if you let me borrow this one."

Frank quickly explained who they were and why they were pursuing the thief. The American agreed to Joe's plan.

As Joe strapped himself into the glider, Frank nervously cautioned him, "I hope you know what you're doing."

Turn to page 98.

From page 59

When they returned to the compartment with the conductor, the Hardys had securely bound Leroux's hands behind his back.

"We have a prisoner to drop off at the next police station," Joe said to the rail official as he tilted his head toward Leroux. "The charge is kidnapping."

The Frenchman stared at Kristy and muttered, "You'll be sorry you betrayed me again!"

Nancy put her arm around her friend's shoulder and led her away from Leroux into an empty compartment.

"It's all over now," she said soothingly. "You'll be safe from him in the future."

"Thanks, Nancy," the young skater said appreciatively. "I'm so glad you came to Innsbruck with me—otherwise . . . " she stopped and shuddered.

"Come on, champ, cheer up," the sleuth said with a smile on her face. "You're headed for the Olympics now."

END

Frank rushed into the rental shop and asked for a pair of cross-country skis and boots. He slung them over his shoulder and hurried outside.

Glancing up the mountain, he saw the man in the fur hat get off the lift. Frank was on one of the chairs a few moments later and began his ascent. During the trip up, he put on his equipment, and by the time he reached the summit he was ready for the pursuit.

He gazed across the mountain, along the cross-country trail that led off from where he stood, and he saw the fugitive in the distance. "That guy has a good head start," Frank murmured to himself. "But he doesn't look like a good skier."

The athletic detective moved quickly across the hard-packed snow. He built up a smooth rhythm on his skis, slowly gaining on the older man in front of him.

The suspect glanced back over his shoulder. The sight of the boy seemed to throw him into a panic, and he dug his posts into the snow and lunged forward.

Several hundred yards ahead, Frank spied a cabin. The sleuth knew he had to catch the skier before he arrived there.

Turn to page 82.

But with a lightning-fast move, Joe threw open the emergency exit door and swung his body out, holding on to the bottom of the car with both hands. Then he gritted his teeth and let go.

The athletic young detective hit the snow with his knees bent and let himself roll, lessening the shock of the impact. Then he hurried out of sight under cover of the darkness. As fast as he could, he ran down the hill.

Above him, the kidnappers angrily yelled orders to the men in the station. Joe had almost reached it when the car began its descent again.

He hurried toward the parking lot and spied a van. "Their getaway car," he said to himself. He glanced at the top of the vehicle, where a luggage rack was covered by a thick tarpaulin.

I have to find out where they're going, Joe thought, and this is my way to do it.

Turn to page 79.

The young detective hoisted himself onto the top of the van and crawled under the tarp. Seconds later, he heard the voices of the kidnappers approaching the car.

"Forget about that kid," the leader was saying. "We'll never find him in the dark. We gotta get out of here!"

Joe felt the doors slam shut after Frank, Kristy, and their captors had climbed into the van. Then he grabbed the luggage rack tightly as the vehicle shot off down the road.

A freezing wind whipped against him as the van traveled at a high speed through the night. When the driver stopped at a railroad crossing, Joe wrapped the tarp around his numbing fingers. Then he huddled down against the warm metal roof for what seemed like an endless ride.

Turn to page 90.

"That might be the same guy we encountered last night!" Nancy speculated. "We'd better follow him!"

The three sleuths jumped into Nancy's Volkswagen and with Frank at the wheel, took off after the snowmobile. He cautiously maneuvered to stay within the tracks cut into the snow by other cars. Ahead of them, the snowmobile seemed to skim over the ground effortlessly.

"I can't go any faster!" the boy said with frustration. "Otherwise, we'll end up in a snowbank."

"Don't worry about it," Nancy assured him. "Our yellow and black fugitive is easy to see against all this white snow. As long as we can keep him in sight, we'll catch up sometime."

The road they were on zigzagged up one of the smaller mountains that rose above Lermoos. Nancy and Joe kept their eyes on the snowmobile as it sped across the winding path directly above them.

Suddenly, from the back seat, Nancy yelled to Frank, "Speed up! A snowslide is coming!"

Turn to page 81.

Frank stepped on the accelerator, staring intently at the road ahead. As the car lunged forward, chunks of snow and ice pounded on the roof.

"Wow!" Joe gasped, looking out the back window. "The road behind us is buried under several feet of powder. We just made it."

"There's only one way to go now," Frank muttered as he clutched the wheel tightly. "Up!"

As he swung the car around a sharp curve, Nancy searched the white landscape in front of them.

"There he is!" she called out, gesturing toward the yellow snowmobile, which was leaving the main road and turning off onto a narrow path. Then it disappeared from sight.

Turn to page 84.

Frank increased his speed, gliding over the snow and getting closer and closer to the man. The suspect turned around again on a downhill stretch.

"Watch out!" the young detective yelled out automatically, seeing the fugitive head straight into a large fir.

But his warning came too late. The man crashed into the tree, then crumpled down onto the snow at its base.

When Frank reached the man, he bent down to examine him. The fugitive had been knocked unconscious, but was still breathing.

"First, I'll see if Kristy's in that cabin," Frank said to himself. "Then, I'll come back to play the good Samaritan."

Quickly, he skied toward the cabin. As he drew nearer, he saw a disturbing sight. A yellow snowmobile with black stripes was parked along the far side of the building!

If you think Frank should go inside the cabin right away, turn to page 87.
If you think he should devise a strategy to get the kidnapper outside, turn to page 96.

Joe pushed the husky assailant down the path to the cable-car station, and informed the excited manager that his prisoner was a kidnapper. The Austrian locked the man inside his office while Joe contacted the police to send a rescue team for the injured criminal. Then the blond sleuth hurried back toward the cabin to see if Frank needed help.

Halfway down the path, he saw his brother and Kristy walking toward him.

"Where's the other guy?" Joe asked curiously as he ran to join them.

"I tied him up in the hut," Frank answered. "He was definitely the brains and not the brawn of the group."

"Kristy, did you find out why they kidnapped you?" the younger Hardy inquired as the three walked in the direction of the cafeteria.

"I just told Frank about it," Kristy replied. "The story is really awful. That man in the cabin is named Ernst Schmidt. During World War II, he watched my father kill his brother in combat in Germany. Later, he was taken as a prisoner of war and found out my father's name. He has been plotting revenge ever since."

Turn to page 117.

Frank drove to the point where they had last seen the vehicle. The small path it had taken was too treacherous for an automobile. The sleuths climbed from their Volkswagen and began to walk through the crunchy snow, following the snowmobile's tracks as they led through tall fir trees.

"I wish I knew where we're going," Joe commented.

"Patience," Frank advised.

The three continued on the trail for fifteen minutes. Then, suddenly, they emerged from the thick pine forest and faced a large, beautiful building.

"A castle!" Nancy exclaimed. "It looks like something out of a fairy tale!"

"Fairy tales can be pretty scary," Joe reminded her. "If Kristy's in there, I hope she's still all right!"

Turn to page 86.

The young detectives slowly crept up to the castle. The yellow and black snowmobile was parked in front of a huge, wooden door.

"Let's circle around to the back," Nancy whispered. "I don't think we should announce our arrival yet."

Frank and Joe followed her lead along a cleared path skirting the stone walls of the building. They walked slowly to avoid making any noise that would disturb the perfect stillness around the castle.

As they rounded a corner that brought them to the back of the castle, they were greeted with a startling sight.

A patio stretched out from the house to a large skating pond, where Kristy Anderson was gliding across the ice with graceful movements. An elderly man in a wheelchair was watching her, an expression of blissful happiness on his face.

Frank, Joe, and Nancy slipped back into hiding behind the stone wall.

"What on earth is going on?" Joe asked in amazement.

"You and Nancy try to find out," Frank said. "I'll try to get into the castle and look for the driver of the snowmobile."

If you want to stay with Joe and Nancy, turn to page 88.
If you want to go inside the castle with Frank, turn to page 91.

Grimly, Frank unstrapped his skis and walked up to the small cabin. He rapped on the door three times.

Several tense minutes passed, and he wondered what was going on inside. He started to turn away to investigate the rear of the dwelling, when suddenly the door swung open and a man lunged at him, pushing him into the snow!

Frank caught a glimpse of his assailant's icy blue eyes as the man jumped on him and reached for his throat.

A wave of anger surged through the boy and gave him extra strength. He thrust the man away with a strong kick and jumped to his feet. A tough fight ensued between the equally matched opponents. They traded punches and wrestled on the icy ground. Finally, Frank landed a blow that knocked his assailant out.

The sleuth rushed through the door. In the cabin, tied to a chair, was Kristy Anderson!

"Oh, Frank," she said admiringly, her blue eyes welling up with tears. "I'm so glad to see you."

Turn to page 108.

Joe and Nancy peered around the corner to take another look at the skating pond. Kristy was performing the routine she had done in the ice arena the night before. The old man seemed mesmerized as he watched her.

"He certainly doesn't look dangerous," Joe said. "Let's find out why Kristy is here."

The two detectives walked out from their hiding place. As they approached the pond, Kristy caught sight of them and came to a sudden stop. She glanced nervously from her friends to the old man, not saying a word.

Her admirer jerked his head up, as though a spell had been broken.

"Who are you?" he demanded of the two visitors as they walked up to him.

"We're friends of Kristy's," Nancy said calmly.

"There is no Kristy here," the old man replied gruffly. "You've interrupted my daughter's skating!"

Turn to page 100.

Joe caught a glimpse of Leroux ahead of him, scrambling down a flight of stairs that led into the Paris Métro, the city's subway system.

The blond detective dodged through the crowd to the steps, taking two at a time. He was only ten yards behind the Frenchman when Leroux reached a platform with a waiting train.

As Leroux ran for it, its doors began to slide shut. He desperately grabbed the two sections, which were inches from meeting in the center, and tried to pry them open. But his efforts were in vain!

The doors slammed together, the train rolled away from the platform, and Joe Hardy grabbed the abductor's two arms from behind.

"This is the end of the line for you," the sleuth said as he led Leroux to the stairs. "The police will be very interested to hear the story Kristy has to tell."

END

Finally, the van came to a stop. Joe kept perfectly still as the passengers got out. He heard the leader giving orders to the others. Then he detected the sound of feet scraping on steps, and, at last, the slam of a shutting door.

Joe stuck his head out from under the tarp. No one was in sight. Quickly he crawled out from his hiding place and dropped down the side of the van. He peered through the darkness at an old farmhouse, where the captors had taken Frank and Kristy. Then he saw a small barn nearby. Cautiously, he ran to the little building and slipped inside to plan his next move and get warm.

For several minutes, Joe paced back and forth, getting the circulation going in his cold body. Meanwhile, he considered his alternatives. He could head out into the darkness in search of a place from where he could call his father. Or, he could creep up to the farmhouse and try to rescue his brother and the young skater.

If you want Joe to attempt a rescue of Frank and Kristy, turn to page 102.
If you think he should try to contact Fenton Hardy, turn to page 104.

After he left Joe and Nancy, Frank crept along the castle wall, looking for an entrance. He came to a small door and opened it stealthily.

Once inside, he moved past the kitchen, where he heard two people talking. He peered around the doorway and noticed an elderly man and woman dressed in servant's uniforms. Cautiously he slipped past them and started up the staircase at the end of the hallway.

He had almost reached the top of the steps when he saw a blond man walking into a room off the hallway.

Silently Frank moved to the door that the man had left open. The stranger stood in front of a large window facing the skating pond.

"Trouble," he muttered to himself. "Those two look like trouble!"

Frank realized that Nancy and Joe must have walked into view. He decided to act quickly.

"Stay where you are," he ordered sternly.

The blond man whirled around to stare at Frank with icy blue eyes.

Turn to page 92.

"It's you again," Frank said calmly. "I remember meeting you in Kristy's dressing room last night."

"How did you follow us here?" the abductor demanded.

"I'll ask the questions," Frank replied angrily. "What's going on?"

"The old count has lost touch with reality," the blond man explained. "He paid me to bring the skater here after he saw her picture in the newspaper. She's the spitting image of his dead daughter, who was also a good skater. Nobody was going to hurt Miss Anderson. All I had to do was collect my money and then take her back to Innsbruck. The count would have thought he had his daughter back for a little while, at least."

"It's not quite that simple!" Frank said. "You can be charged with abducting Kristy against her will. You'd better start cooperating with us if you don't want to spend a lot of time in jail."

A look of fear flashed over the man's face, and he nodded in agreement.

The young detective went to the window and saw Joe and Nancy walking into the castle with Kristy.

"You were playing a dangerous game," he said to the abductor. "Thank goodness it's all over without Kristy's being hurt!"

END

After the police had left with Mr. Becker, Nancy took a taxi to the hotel where Kristy was staying with her coach. When the young skater saw her friend, she greeted her with exciting news.

"Frank and Joe got my medal back! I just spoke with them on the phone. They didn't explain the details. But they said they'd bring it to me later tonight."

"That's terrific!" the sleuth replied with a broad smile. "And wait till you hear the story *I* have to tell!"

END

By 9:55, Nancy was back on the street in front of Leroux's apartment house, her plan ready to go into action. A short time later, she spied a taxi driving slowly up the well-lit street. It stopped in front of No. 182 and Jacques Leroux climbed from the back seat, pulling Kristy out after him. The sleuth saw the frightened expression on her friend's face. Then she walked calmly toward her.

"Excusez-moi," Nancy said.

The young skater stared at the stranger, whose face was shaded by a large hat. Then recognition dawned on her. Leroux was busy paying the cab driver and didn't take notice of the disguised detective.

Nancy opened her map of Paris, explaining that she was lost. Kristy moved closer to her friend, edging away from Leroux. As the young Frenchman turned away from the taxi toward Kristy, Nancy made her move.

She grabbed the skater's arm and ran with her down the street. Meanwhile, a Paris gendarme jumped from a car parked nearby and rushed at Leroux.

Turn to page 95.

Nancy turned around when she heard the young Frenchman's scream of rage. He had been safely captured by the strong gendarme, who was now pushing him into the unmarked police car.

"You're safe, Kristy," the young sleuth assured her friend as she pulled off her hat. "The authorities know all about Leroux. When Frank and Joe arrive, we'll go to the police station to make out a report."

"Nancy, you're incredible!" the blond skater said shakily. "I was more scared than I've ever been in my whole life!"

"You're the one who is incredible, Kristy," the titian-haired detective replied. "Not only did you skate a perfect figure-eight—you left a perfect clue in it as well!"

END

Frank's first impulse was to barge into the cabin right away to see if Kristy was there. But, instead, he unstrapped his skis and slipped behind a tree to devise a strategy. As he gazed down at the hard-packed snow around him, he remembered all the snowball fights he'd been in. He realized he had a limitless supply of potential weapons—right at his feet!

He set to work, molding the snow into hard, compact balls. He stacked them in a pile behind a thick tree that was in good throwing range of the cabin. When he had made twenty balls, he picked one up and sent it smashing into the door.

Frank waited thirty seconds, then threw another one. He realized that whoever was inside the cabin wouldn't know what was hitting the door. Sooner or later, they would have to investigate. And he was ready.

The sleuth pitched a third and fourth ball at the building. Then, the moment he was waiting for arrived. A blond-haired man opened the door and peered out, his eyes squinting at the bright sun. Frank whizzed an icy ball straight at his head. It landed on target perfectly. The man, stunned by the impact, staggered.

Turn to page 97.

Frank sprinted to the door and took his victim by surprise. He landed a punch on the man's jaw and twisted his arms behind his back. Then he dragged him into the cabin, where he saw the frightened face of Kristy Anderson!

"Frank, it's you!" she said with relief. "I didn't know what was attacking this place."

"Kristy, I have to tie this guy up quickly. Can you find some rope?"

The young skater did, then assisted Frank in restraining the struggling abductor, who stared at the young detective with icy blue eyes.

"We had the perfect setup," he snarled. "How did you find us?"

"You made the mistake of mentioning Lermoos to her when you took her. Kristy left us a clue," Frank told him. "The rest was a simple case of the good guys beating the bad guys."

A smile of admiration came over Kristy's face as Frank led her outside.

"Now let's tie up the other guy over there," the boy said. "I think he just came back from leaving a ransom note in Igles."

Kristy took a deep breath of the fresh mountain air. "It feels so good to be free again!" she exclaimed. "Thanks, Frank. You deserve a gold medal for this!"

END

"So do I." Joe grinned and stepped onto the rock ledge. Then he made a running leap into the air, soaring after the red glider below him.

As Joe looked at Innsbruck from his dizzying bird's-eye view, he realized he had never flown a glider from such a height. The cold air cut into his face as he floated on the wind currents. He tried to follow the fugitive's course through the sky, manipulating his steering mechanism carefully.

"I'm going to make it down," the young sleuth whispered to himself for courage as he glanced back at the rocky mountain slope. He knew he had to avoid an air current that might smash him into its side.

The two gliders swooped through the sky, slowly losing altitude. As Joe came nearer the ground, he gained confidence. His hang-gliding instructor had always said he was excellent at landings.

He saw that the other glider was headed for an open meadow, and readied himself for landing as the assailant hit the ground below him.

Turn to page 99.

Then, with a plop, Joe's body settled into the blanket of snow.

For some seconds he was stunned by the impact. Then he unstrapped his body from the glider and got to his feet. A couple of hundred yards away, he saw the red glider resting on the snow. Yet, its pilot hadn't moved from his landing spot!

Weary from his flight, Joe plodded through the snow. As he drew nearer to the assailant, he saw that the man's face was twisted with pain.

"Help me," the fugitive begged. "My leg may be broken. I can't walk."

Joe gazed down at Kristy's abductor. "Hand over the medal," he demanded. "Then I'll get an ambulance."

With an agonized groan, the man reached into his jacket and pulled out the skater's prize.

Turn to page 107.

Nancy and Joe looked at each other curiously. Then they turned to their young friend, who had come up to the edge of the pond near them.

"This is my daughter, Katja," the man announced. "She will become the greatest skater in the world."

As Joe opened his mouth to protest, Kristy stopped him with a whispered plea.

"Don't try to argue with him. Nothing I've said has changed his mind."

The young detectives finally understood Kristy's strange predicament. The owner of the castle was living in a dream world of his own making. He seemed to be totally convinced that Kristy was his daughter. Nancy decided to play along with his game.

"We've come to talk with Katja," she said. "It's about her next competition."

"Very well, very well," the old man said, motioning them to go inside. "As long as it's about her skating."

Kristy hurriedly put on her skate guards and led Joe and Nancy into a room off the patio.

"Thank goodness you're here!" she said shakily. "I haven't been hurt. But I want to get back to reality as soon as possible!"

Turn to page 101.

At that moment, Frank Hardy entered the room, pushing a blond-haired, blue-eyed man in front of him.

"This is the man we saw in Kristy's dressing room!" Nancy exclaimed.

"He forced me to go with him from Igles this morning," Kristy said angrily. "He told me someone in Lermoos wanted to see me. I started to leave a clue—"

"We found it, Kristy," Nancy replied. Then she turned to the blond man. "Now please tell us what is going on here!"

"My father saw Miss Anderson's picture in the newspaper last week," he said. "She does have an uncanny resemblance to my late sister. He asked me to bring her here, and . . . to make him happy for a moment, I did. I was going to take her back to Innsbruck tonight. No one was going to harm her. Please, you must believe me!"

Kristy glanced out the window at the old man.

"It's so sad, isn't it?" she murmured. "He lost his daughter but thought he could bring her back to life."

"Perhaps he has," Nancy replied. "In his mind."

"I'll try to talk to him again," Kristy decided. "Maybe it will make him happy if I promise to visit him whenever I'm in Austria."

Joe smiled. "That way our fairy tale would have a happy ending, after all!"

END

Joe decided to check out the farmhouse. He knew the kidnappers would have to go to sleep sometime; he hoped for a chance to catch them off guard.

The young sleuth crept through the darkness up to the old stone building. A light was shining in a front room. He pressed his body against a wall as another light flicked on near him. Cautiously, he peeked through the window and saw Frank and Kristy being shoved into a small bedroom. Their hands had been tied behind their backs.

Joe waited until the kidnapper had switched off the light and left the room. Then he softly tapped a signal on the windowpane that he and Frank had used since childhood.

A minute later, he heard someone on the other side trying to unlatch the lock. Suddenly, the window opened.

"Joe?" Frank whispered in surprise.

"Yes," Joe replied. "Give me your hands and I'll cut you loose."

He pulled out his Swiss Army knife and cut Frank's bonds. Then Frank freed Kristy.

"Let's get out of here!" The dark-haired Hardy said urgently as he helped Kristy through the window. "There's something I've got to tell Dad!"

Turn to page 112.

From page 90

Joe decided to contact his father as soon as possible. The stakes were too high for him to try to free Frank and Kristy on his own and possibly fail.

He set off down the road, jogging at a steady pace. He didn't know where he was going to or coming from, but he kept a mental note of how far he traveled.

Within fifteen minutes, Joe arrived at another farmhouse. He walked up to the darkened building and knocked on the door. A short time later, a light flicked on and a sleepy-eyed man appeared.

"I need to use a telephone," Joe quickly explained.

"Ich spreche kaum Englisch," the man replied.

Joe repeated his request in halting German. Even though he knew the language well, he had become a bit rusty of late.

The man eyed the young sleuth curiously, then led him into the house to a telephone.

Joe immediately dialed his father's number in Geneva. A worried Fenton Hardy answered on the other end. He explained that Nancy had contacted him about the boys' disappearance, and Joe quickly told him all the day's events.

Turn to page 109.

Nancy took Kristy's arm and led her down the stairs. They could hear Joe still arguing with the men in the front room as they ran out the rear door.

"Get on the snowmobile!" Nancy ordered Kristy.

Just then, a gust of wind slammed the door shut behind them.

"What's going on?" one of the men yelled from inside.

Nancy jumped on the snowmobile, turned the ignition key, and stepped hard on the accelerator. The vehicle shot across the snow as the two men rushed to the door.

"Hold on tight, Kristy!" the detective yelled and steered the small vehicle around a stand of trees onto the road. Running toward them at full speed was Joe Hardy. He jumped on behind Kristy as Nancy slowed down. Then the three sped off to the ski station.

"They're following us!" Joe shouted after he saw the two men jump into the Mercedes.

Turn to page 106.

Nancy kept the gas pedal down all the way until she saw the ski station on the left. She steered the snowmobile right up to the hut. When the three young Americans jumped off and ran for the door, the Mercedes shot by on the road.

"They're trying to make a getaway," Joe exclaimed. "I'll call the police."

Kristy almost collapsed on the steps as she and the titian-haired detective went to the hut.

"Was I glad to see you!" she said in a trembling voice. "How did you find me?"

"I saw your clue in the ice," Nancy explained. "The rest was just good luck."

"That guy on the snowmobile took me away," the skater said. "He was foolish enough to mention Lermoos. But I never thought you'd find me from a three-letter clue. I had no time to finish the word."

Joe came back from the phone booth. "The police are already after the kidnappers," he reported. "Those guys'll get a hundred years in jail rather than a hundred thousand dollars in ransom money!"

"What!" Kristy said in amazement. "They asked for that much?"

Nancy laughed and hugged her friend. "You're worth every cent of it!" she said.

END

Four hours later, Joe was wrapped in blankets in his hotel room. Frank, Nancy, and Kristy sat on the bed around him discussing the solution to the gold-medal theft.

"Mr. Becker told the police that he was a paid spy, smuggling information to hostile countries on his gold work," Nancy explained. "He decided to confess to the authorities after his contact, Kristy's abductor, tried to kill him."

"Your gold medal has coded information on it, Kristy," Frank added. "Another country expected its skater to win the competition and bring the medal back. When you won, its agents had to steal it."

"This morning, that medal meant everything to me," the young skater said thoughtfully. "Tonight, I'm just happy that we're all alive and well."

"Me, too," Joe murmured drowsily as his eyes slowly closed.

Nancy smiled down at the blond-haired detective. Then she whispered, "Let's go. The hero needs some sleep."

END

"Are you okay?" he asked with concern as he freed the young skater.

Kristy nodded, then followed Frank outside, where he bound the blond man's hands and legs.

"There's another guy over there," Frank said, pointing to the spot where the older man was slumped in the snow. "But he's not going anywhere."

The dark-haired detective put his arm around Kristy's shoulder and led her back into the cabin.

"Nancy found your clue in the ice," he said. "She guessed it might mean Lermoos."

"That guy on the snowmobile forced me to go with him this morning," Kristy explained. "First, he tried to get me to come on my own by saying my coach needed me in Lermoos."

"The older man must have just come back from Igles," Frank speculated. "Eric found a ransom note at the hotel this afternoon."

"I wonder what they might have done with me," Kristy shuddered, "if it hadn't been for you."

Frank couldn't find the words to describe how he felt. Instead, he just held Kristy tight.

At that moment, Joe and Nancy appeared at the door. "We called the hotel and since there was no news, we rented skis and followed the cross-country trail here. We came to offer our help," Joe explained.

Nancy grinned. "He doesn't need any. Looks as if your brother has things well under control!"

END

"Where are you now, son?" Fenton Hardy asked.

"You speak German, Dad. This man I'm with will tell you my location."

Joe handed the telephone to the surprised farmer, who informed Mr. Hardy that he lived near Bregenz, Austria. After the investigator got the directions from the man, he asked to speak to Joe again.

"I'll call the local police and explain the situation," he said. "You wait where you are. The detectives will be by to pick you up before they attempt to rescue Frank and Kristy."

"Okay, Dad," Joe said with relief. "Good-bye for now."

While he waited for the authorities, the farmer offered him some food, which Joe ate with great relish. By the time two police cars pulled up, the young sleuth had a full stomach of sausage and potatoes.

Joe joined the team of six officers, who had discussed a strategy with Fenton Hardy for the rescue attempt. They drove to the farmhouse where Frank and Kristy were being held captive.

Turn to page 114.

He followed the tracks of the two skiers, who were several hundred yards ahead of him, and zigzagged down the hill with ease, worried about his friend.

If she fell and broke her leg, he murmured to himself, it could mean the end of her skating career.

Just then the kidnapper turned around and spotted their pursuer. He pulled Kristy along the treacherous hill at a faster pace.

Frank decided he had to act quickly. He gave a hard push with his poles and shot forward, going straight downhill at a high speed. When he neared the other skiers, he took both poles in his left hand and swerved to the side of the kidnapper. As he shot by, he reached out his right arm and grabbed hold of the man's jacket.

Turn to page 111.

The kidnapper was jerked away from Kristy. He flailed about until he finally lost his balance and crashed into the snow, injuring his ankle and grabbing it in pain.

Frank stopped and rushed to Kristy, who had come to a wobbly halt.

"I'm okay," the young skater said in a trembling voice. Then she added with relief, "At least I didn't break a leg!"

Turn to page 116.

The three friends dashed away from the farmhouse into the darkness. As they jogged down the road the van had come by, Frank excitedly told Joe what he had overheard.

"Those guys have planted a bomb in the new atomic research center outside Geneva," he explained. "Dad has been hired to investigate the possibility of sabotage there. We have to tell him about the explosive before it goes off!"

About half an hour later, Frank, Joe, and Kristy arrived at a *gasthaus* that was still serving customers. Frank rushed to the pay telephone and dialed his father's number.

Turn to page 113.

"I was just ready to leave for Innsbruck," Mr. Hardy told him. "Nancy telephoned me that you hadn't returned from your investigation of a kidnapping."

"We were kidnapped, too," Frank said with a chuckle. "But, thanks to Joe, we're all okay. Listen, Dad, there's something really important I have to tell you."

"Yes?"

Frank gave his father the details of the criminals' plot against the atomic research center.

"I'll get over there right away!" Fenton Hardy exclaimed. "You call the local police and ask them to take Kristy back. I'll contact the chief inspector of the area and have him send some men to join you. With your help, they may be able to round up the saboteurs tonight."

Turn to page 115.

Joe and the six officers stopped some distance from the building. Then they stealthily crept up and surrounded it. On a given signal from their radios, the officers broke down both the front and back doors and rushed inside. Joe followed cautiously behind them.

The police quickly captured the kidnappers, all of whom were caught sleeping. Joe rushed into a small bedroom and found Frank and Kristy groggily trying to understand what was happening.

"Thanks, Joe," the older Hardy said as his brother cut the ropes around his wrists. "You really saved the day."

END

Within twenty minutes, the local police came to escort the young skater back to her hotel. Frank had called Nancy to let her know Kristy would be arriving. A short time later, a team of detectives pulled up. The two Hardys hopped in one of their cars and directed them to the old farmhouse.

The officers ordered Frank and Joe to stay put as they prepared to raid the building. The young sleuths watched as their former captors were taken by surprise, handcuffed, and locked inside a police van.

Frank and Joe rode back to the station house with the detectives. From there, they contacted Fenton Hardy at the atomic research center. The famous investigator had used a trained dog to snoop out the explosive. Then a team of experts had defused the bomb.

"What a day!" Frank exclaimed as he put down the telephone.

"What a night!" Joe added. "Twenty-four hours ago, we were worried about Kristy disappearing. It turned out that she was a pawn in an even more dangerous game than kidnapping."

He paused and rubbed his hand over his empty stomach. "Frank," he asked. "Do you think we could get something to eat now?"

END

That evening, Kristy and the three young detectives gathered in a restaurant in Igles to discuss the incredible events of the day.

"Those crooks will be a terrible embarrassment to their country," Joe commented. "They confessed they had kidnapped Kristy to keep her out of next week's competition in London. They figured their skater would have a better chance of winning if Kristy wasn't there."

"I was worried that I'd never compete again," Kristy added with a shudder. "I thought I'd crash into a tree on those skis for sure."

"I'm sorry I wasn't there to help," Nancy chimed in. "I feel as though I missed out on all the excitement."

"You want excitement?" Joe asked with a grin. "How about a downhill skiing race tomorrow?"

"Great!" the titian-blond sleuth answered. "The loser buys dinner tomorrow night."

"And who's buying tonight?" Frank asked jokingly.

"I am," Nancy replied, "for one gold-medal skater and two heroes of the day!"

END

"What was he planning to do with you?" Joe asked anxiously.

"I'm not sure," Kristy said with a shudder. "But I'm glad I didn't find out. He'd hired that blond man to kidnap me from the skating pond this morning. They'd made two attempts the night before. I think they were going to take me somewhere else and then send a ransom note to my father."

"The police will take care of them," Frank reassured the skater. "You don't have to worry that Ernst Schmidt will ever bother you again."

"Thanks so much for your help," Kristy said to the young detectives, with tears in her eyes. "You risked your lives for me."

Joe shrugged off the compliment with a smile. "It was all in the line of duty. Now let's get back to Igles," he added. "I know a friend of yours down there who will be very happy to see you again."

END

The Hardy Boys®
Mystery Stories

by Franklin W. Dixon

There are many exciting Hardy Boys Mysteries in Armada. Have you read these thrilling adventures?

The Mystery of the Melted Coins (7)

The young detectives find themselves in big trouble when they tangle with a cut-throat modern-day pirate.

The Shore Road Mystery (17)

The Hardys are determined to clear the names of their friends who are accused of a series of car thefts. But the boys soon find themselves at the mercy of the deadly, web-spinning spider man . . .

The Crimson Flame (75)

The Hardy Boys' hunt for a gang of jewel thieves takes them deep into the treacherous jungles of Thailand — and into a terrifying trap . . .

Cave-In (76)

The boys travel into the snow-covered mountains in search of a kidnapped actor. But they soon stumble on a far weirder mystery . . .

Armada

Nancy Drew®
Mystery Stories

by Carolyn Keene

Have you read all the books in this thrilling series?
Here are a few of the titles available:

The Clue in the Crossword Cipher (5)

Nancy travels to the mountains of Peru in search of price-
less treasure. But she soon discovers that an unknown
enemy is determined to stop her . . .

The Whispering Statue (14)

The eerie statue of the Whispering Girl points Nancy to an
ancient mystery that haunts the decaying Old Estate. But
horror awaits her in the night . . .

The Triple Hoax (51)

An invitation to a display of magic puts Nancy on the
track of a ruthless gang of con men. But she soon realizes
that the tricksters are dangerous criminals . . .

The Silver Cobweb (65)

A mysterious spider symbol is Nancy's only clue to a jewel
robbery. But she quickly becomes enmeshed in a terrifying web of danger . . .

Armada

The Hardy Boys®
Ghost Stories

by Franklin W. Dixon

Six chilling mysteries

The Hardy Boys are experts at solving mysteries that have the police baffled. But the adversaries they tackle now are no mere mortals. Ghostly spirits from another world haunt Frank and Joe with blood-freezing fear . . .

The ghastly scarecrow that stalks the night . . . A haunted castle, cursed by witches . . . The phantom ship that sails to doom . . .

Dare you face them?

Armada

The Beggar's Curse
by Ann Cheetham

Is there no escape from the village of evil?

When Colin, Oliver and Prill arrive in Stang they realize
at once that something is wrong with the village. Up on
the surrounding hills spring is blossoming, but in this dark
little valley no flowers bloom and birds never sing.

Prill knows there is something sinister about the age-old
rituals of the village play. Colin knows the gruesome
incidents that keep happening are no accidents. But Oliver
alone knows the awful secret of Stang and sees the ancient
evil rising from the black waters of Blake's Pit. He feels
the terrible power of the beggarman's curse . . .

The Beggar's Curse is a chilling sequel to *Black Harvest*,
which was chosen in a special selection by British children
as one of their favourite books in 1984. One reader said of
it: "It was like opening a fridge door . . ."

Armada

Here are just a few of the best-selling titles that Armada has to offer:

☐ The Beggar's Curse *Ann Cheetham* £1.25
☐ Cave-In *Franklin W. Dixon* £1.25
☐ Little Men *Louisa M. Alcott* £1.00
☐ The Boy Next Door *Enid Blyton* £1.25
☐ The Phantom of Dark Oaks *Ann Sheldon* £1.25
☐ Theodora and the Chalet School
   Elinor M. Brent-Dyer £1.25
☐ Heidi *Johanna Spyri* 95p
☐ Indiana Jones & the Temple of Doom Storybook £2.95
☐ The Spookster's Handbook *Peter Eldin* £1.25
☐ The Gateway of Doom *J. H. Brennan* £1.50

Armadas are available in bookshops and newsagents, but can also be ordered by post.

HOW TO ORDER
ARMADA BOOKS, Cash Sales Dept., GPO Box 29, Douglas, Isle of Man. British Isles. Please send purchase price plus 15p per book (maximum postal charge £3.00) Customers outside the UK also send purchase price plus 15p per book. Cheque, postal or money order — no currency.

NAME (Block letters) _____

ADDRESS _____

_____

_____